Hold On!

Elspeth Graham

Illustrated by Kate Simpson

FAMILY LEARNING

Hippo found a skateboard.

She got on it.

Whoosh! Off she went.

Hippo met Giraffe.

Giraffe got on.

"Hold on!" said Hippo.

Whoosh! Off they went.

Monkey got on.

Whoosh! They went very fast
"Hold on!"
cried all the monkeys.

Parrot got on.

Whoosh! They went too fast.

"Hold on!"
cried all the animals.

"Stop!" said Rhino.

But they could not stop.

"Stop!" said Gorilla.

But they could not stop.

"Help!" they all cried.
"We can't stop!"

Splash!
They went into the river.

"That was lucky!" they said.

Picture Words

hippo

giraffe

monkey

parrot

rhino

gorilla

skateboard

river